I ♥ cat

Abuelita is the coolest

JK & SM: To all the little brown hands holding this book.

SM: To my razzle-dazzle pink maman, Mehri;
you've always been my personal hero.

MM: Dedicated to A, O, and D.
May you always be proud of your color.

Published by Familius LLC, www.familius.com
PO Box 1249, Reedley, CA 93654

Familius books are available at special discounts for bulk purchases, whether for sales promotions or for family or corporate use. For more information, contact Familius Sales at orders@familius.com. Reproduction of this book in any manner, in whole or in part, without written permission of the publisher is prohibited.

Library of Congress Control Number: 2021935538
Print ISBN 978-1-64170-578-3
Ebook ISBN 978-1-64170-597-4
FE 978-1-64170-611-7
KF 978-1-64170-625-4
Printed in China

Edited by Brooke Jorden with Bobby Lee Mireles, advisor
Cover and book design by Brooke Jorden

10 9 8 7 6 5 4 3 2 1

First Edition

THE PROUDEST COLOR!

I am like a box of crayons—
bright and colorful. I see and
feel in color.

When I am **HAPPY**, I feel a rush of razzle-dazzle pink in my hands.

When I am **MAD**, I feel sparks of bright red spread across my cheeks.

When I am **SAD**, I feel a deep blue in my eyes.

When I am **NERVOUS**, I feel a vivid purple in my stomach.

When I am **PROUD**, I feel a beautiful brown in my heart. But, for me, brown is more than feeling proud.

It's the color I see when I see **ME.**

It's the color that people see when I come into a room,

get on the bus,

or go to the store.

It's the color on my arms,
my toes, and my face!

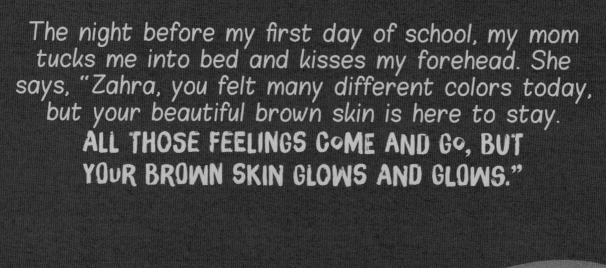

The night before my first day of school, my mom tucks me into bed and kisses my forehead. She says, "Zahra, you felt many different colors today, but your beautiful brown skin is here to stay. ALL THOSE FEELINGS COME AND GO, BUT YOUR BROWN SKIN GLOWS AND GLOWS."

I press my arm against my mom's,
and I like seeing the differences and
similarities in our shades of brown.

On my first day of school, I feel razzle-dazzle pink **HAPPY** and vivid purple **NERVOUS** when my mom drops me off.

But the people here are not like my box of crayons. They might have colorful feelings inside, but I am the only one who is brown on the outside.

I stare at my brown arms
and remember my mom's words:
MY BROWN SKIN GLOWS AND GLOWS.

I feel a rush of brown **PRIDE** in my chest and march into my classroom, radiating sunshine yellow CONFIDENCE.

At recess, my classmate Zoey presses her arm against mine, wrinkles her nose, and says, "You're so dark. I don't like brown." Everyone laughs. I stare at our arms and feel many colors swirl inside me.

I feel bright red ANGER in my cheeks
and deep blue SADNESS in my eyes,
but I don't feel brown pride inside my chest.
In that moment, I wish I wasn't brown on the outside.

At dinner, I tell my parents what happened at school. My mom and papá tell me that there are people who can be mean when they see my beautiful brown skin because it is different from their skin.

"But we want you to remember all the people who share your brown skin and all the important things they have done in this world.

Brown is the color of your **ABUELA**, who loves to hug and kiss you.

It is the color of your old school **PRINCIPAL**, who high-fived the students as he walked down the hallway.

It is the color of your **DOCTOR**, who helps you feel better when you are sick.

It is the color of **MARTIN LUTHER KING JR.**, who inspired America with his dream of equality.

It is the color of **MALALA YOUSAFZAI**, who bravely stands up for all girls to be able to go to school.

It is the color of **CÉSAR CHÁVEZ**, who helped workers have safe and fair places to work.

It is the color of former President **BARACK OBAMA**, who helped keep our country safe and strong.

It is the color of **KAMALA HARRIS**, who is the first woman to become Vice President of our country, and said that she wouldn't be the last.

It is the color of **FRIDA KAHLO**, who boldly painted her culture and brought attention to female artists like you. All these people have beautiful brown skin like yours."

As they tell me about each of these brown and beautiful people, I feel a rush of razzle-dazzle pink spread in my hands.

Even though I might be the only kid with brown skin in school, I am part of a very special box of crayons. This box is full of amazing people from all around the world and all throughout history who are brown like me.

No matter what Zoey says, my brown skin is important, and it's a color that makes a big difference in the world. It's the color that I am, and I will make a difference in the world.

I see **BROWN** all over my skin.
I feel **BROWN** fill my heart.
I FEEL PROUD!

A Note to Parents and Caregivers

"If I pulled it off, kids all over the world would see themselves and their possibilities differently. And that alone would be worth it."

—BARACK OBAMA

Cultural socialization—the promotion of cultural, ethnic, and racial pride—can help build a child's positive racial identity in the face of discrimination.[1] After Zahra experiences discrimination, her parents use this concept to remind her of all the important people who share her skin color and all of the inspiring things they have done. By age 5, children often share the same racial attitudes of their parents and caregivers, so it is critical to have conversations about race and racism early and often. Avoiding discussing these topics may send the message that they are not important or even taboo, when the home should be a safe place to have these conversations. We hope the following recommendations can help facilitate these conversations with your child:

Check in with yourself. Before having a conversation, clarify what you want your child to take away from it. Also, take a moment to assess any challenges you may have with this conversation; examine internal biases or stereotypes that you may hold.

Ask open-ended questions. Remember that this isn't just one long conversation, but rather an ongoing dialogue with your child. Use open-ended questions to elicit more detailed responses: "What is the difference between *fair* and *unfair*?" or "When was a time something was done to you or someone else that you felt was unfair?" Children ages 5–8 can understand the concept of fairness and equality, and you can use this understanding as an avenue to discuss how communities of color have been treated unfairly.

Read diverse children's books. Books like *The Proudest Color* as well as other children's books on race, racism, diversity, social justice, and multiculturalism are an excellent entry to discussing these topics. Children readily relate to characters in books, and open-ended questions you could ask while reading these books together include: "What do you think it was like for Zahra on her first day of school?" or "When was a time that you felt like Zahra?"

Be genuine and model respect. You don't need to have answers to every question, but show your child you are open to learning together. Your child will imitate your behaviors and your beliefs, even when you are not in front of them! Use this as an opportunity to model an attitude of openness and respect toward others.

Model healthy expression of emotions. Your child may feel a range of emotions after experiencing discrimination or learning about it. Express to children that feelings are normal and that it is okay for them to feel sad, mad, or frustrated. As adults, we can model healthy expressions of feelings and how to cope with big feelings, including labeling them, taking a break, deep breathing, or writing or drawing about it.

Modulate media. Because the media and news often portray communities of color negatively, consciously share with your child diverse content with a wide range of characters and positive depictions. Additionally, too much exposure to news coverage can lead to negative mental health effects, especially for young children. By limiting exposure, we are not trying to ignore the truth, but parents and caregivers can instead facilitate age-appropriate conversations about current events.

Instill hope. Close the conversation with your child with a discussion on hope. Remind them that change is happening and that people are working together to make the world a better place. Tie the past to the present by discussing the work of great civil rights heroes who helped pave the road forward by advocating for fairness and equality for all. Engage your child in advocacy work, such as contacting political leaders together or volunteering for organizations that promote diversity, equity, and inclusion.

For more resources to support your family
and facilitate cultural socialization, visit our website at

www.theproudestcolor.com

1. Hughes, D. (2003). Correlates of African American and Latino parents' messages to children about ethnicity and race: A comparative study of racial socialization. *American Journal of Community Psychology*, 31(1-2), 15-33.

Dear Zahra,
The teacher told me what I said was wrong and that brown is beautiful. I'm sorry I was mean to you.
♡ Zoey

To: Zahra ❀

ME + ZOEY

Dear Zoey,
BROWN is AWESOME!
(examples below)
trees
ice cream
violins
my cat!
ME!
Love, Zahra

Jadav Payeng

Nelson Mandela

PEACE

Mae Jemison

Christiane Amanpour

News